STEP-BY-STEP
EXPERIMENTS WITH THE
WATER CYCLE

By Shirley Duke

Illustrated by Bob Ostrom

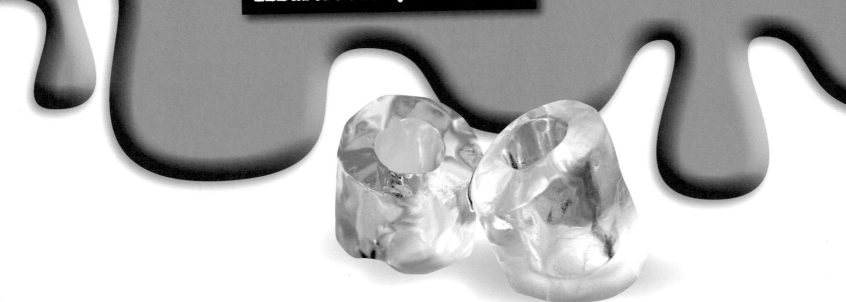

The Child's World

Published by The Child's World®
1980 Lookout Drive • Mankato, MN 56003-1705
800-599-READ • www.childsworld.com

ACKNOWLEDGMENTS
The Child's World®: Mary Berendes, Publishing Director
The Design Lab: Design and production
Red Line Editorial: Editorial direction
Consultant: Diane Bollen, Project Coordinator, Mars Rover Mission,
   Cornell University

ISBN 9781609736156
LCCN 2011940151

PHOTO CREDITS
Konstantin Sutyagin/Shutterstock Images, cover; Pilar Echeverria/
Dreamstime, cover, back cover; Sarunez/Dreamstime, 1, 16; Serghei
Velusceac/Shutterstock Images, 4; Brykaylo Yuriy/Shutterstock Images,
8; Jeremy Reds/Dreamstime, 10; Konstantin Kirillov/Shutterstock Images,
14; Andrey Armyagov/Shutterstock Images, 18; DinaDesign/Shutter-
stock Images, 23; Shutterstock Images, 28

Design elements: Pilar Echeverria/Dreamstime, Robisklp/Dreamstime,
Sarit Saliman/Dreamstime, Jeffrey Van Daele/Dreamstime

Printed in the United States of America

BE SAFE!

The experiments in this book are meant for kids to do themselves. Sometimes an adult's help is needed though. Look in the supply list for each experiment. It will list if an adult is needed. Also, some supplies will need to be bought by an adult.

TABLE OF CONTENTS

4

The sun, clouds, and rain make up the water cycle.

CHAPTER ONE

Study the Water Cycle!

Did you know Earth recycles its water? All the water in the world has been here a long time. You might be drinking the water a dinosaur once drank! The amount of water on Earth does not change. That is because it moves in a cycle.

The sun shines on oceans, ponds, lakes, and rivers. Its heat changes the water from a liquid to **water vapor**. Tiny drops of water move into the air. Water in the air rises high into the sky. This makes clouds. Water falls from clouds as rain, hail, or snow. It falls on all parts of the earth. Water on Earth's surface forms streams and rivers. The water collects in ponds, lakes, and oceans. Some water soaks into the ground. This is **groundwater**.

This cycle keeps going as water moves from air to land and back. How can you learn more about the water cycle?

CHAPTER TWO

Seven Science Steps

Doing a science **experiment** is a fun way to discover new facts!
An experiment follows steps to find answers to science questions.
This book has experiments to help you learn about the water
cycle. You will follow the same seven steps in each experiment:

Seven Steps

1. Research: Figure out the facts before you get started.

2. Question: What do you want to learn?

3. Guess: Make a **prediction**. What do you think will happen in the experiment?

4. Gather: Find the supplies you need for your experiment.

5. Experiment: Follow the directions.

6. Review: Look at the results of the experiment.

7. Conclusion: The experiment is done. Now it is time to reach a **conclusion**. Was your prediction right?

Are you ready to become a scientist? Let's experiment to learn about the water cycle!

8

Does water from a lake go into the air?

CHAPTER THREE

Water on the Move

Water is a liquid, but it can change forms. How does this happen? Try this experiment to see.

Research the Facts

Here are a few. What else do you know?

- Water in the air is water vapor. It is so small you cannot see it.
- Water **evaporates** to become water vapor.

Ask Questions

- Where does water go when it dries up?
- Is a certain temperature needed for water to evaporate?

Make a Prediction

Here are two examples:

- Water evaporates faster in the heat.
- Water evaporates faster in the shade.

Gather Your Supplies!

- 2 small flat bowls
- Water
- Teaspoon
- A sunny window
- A shady spot
- Pencil or pen
- Paper

Time to Experiment!

1. Set out the small, flat bowls. Put them side-by-side.

2. Add 2 teaspoons of water to each bowl.

3. Put one bowl in direct sunlight.

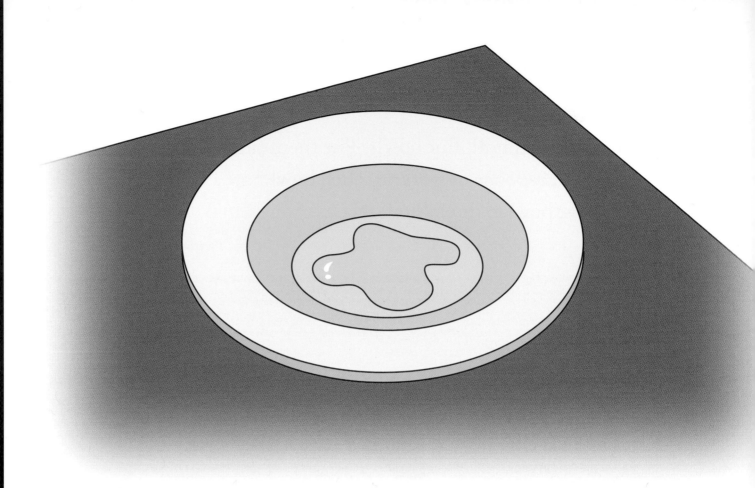

4. Put the other bowl in a shady spot.
5. Check the bowls every four hours until you go to sleep.
   Write down what happens.
6. Check the bowls in the morning. Write down what you see.

Review the Results

Read your notes. What did you notice about the water? There was less water in the bowl in the sunny window. There was more water in the bowl in the shady spot.

What Is Your Conclusion?

The water in the sunny bowl evaporated. The sun's heat made it change to water vapor. The shady spot had a lower temperature. High temperatures make water evaporate faster than low temperatures.

Have you dried your hands on a blow dryer? The hot air speeds up the evaporation. This dries them quickly.

14

Can ice help you see water vapor?

CHAPTER FOUR

Water from the Air

Water vapor is all around us in the air. It is hard to see, though. Is there a way to see water in the air? This experiment will show you.

Research the Facts

Here are a few. What other facts can you find?

- **Condensation** in the air makes clouds.
- Water vapor rises high into the sky.

Ask Questions

- What makes water vapor turn back into liquid?
- Does the temperature change water vapor?

Make a Prediction

Here are two examples.

- Cooling makes water vapor change back to a liquid.
- Cooling water vapor does not change it.

- A drinking glass
- Water
- Ice cubes
- Pencil or pen
- Paper

Gather Your Supplies!

Time to Experiment!

1. Fill a dry glass with ice cubes.
2. Add water until the glass is almost full.
3. Wait 30 minutes.

4. Check the glass. Write down what you see.

5. Slide your finger over the outside of the glass. What do you feel?

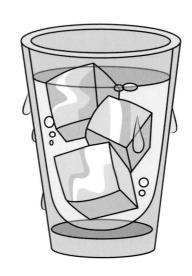

Review the Results

What happened after 30 minutes? You probably saw water outside the glass. You did not spill any water, though.

What Is Your Conclusion?

The cold water in the glass cooled the air around it. This cooled some of the water vapor in the air, too. When water vapor cools down, it turns back into liquid form. The water on the outside of the glass was water vapor just 30 minutes ago. Cool temperatures change water vapor into liquid.

Have you touched grass in the morning? It is wet! That is dew. It is water vapor that has turned back into water because of the cool air.

18

Rain is precipitation that falls from clouds.

CHAPTER FIVE

Make It Rain!

Rain is a big part of the water cycle. How does it fall from clouds in the sky? Try this experiment to see.

Research the Facts

Here are a few. What else do you know?

- Steam is water vapor.
- Clouds are high in the sky. The higher you go in the sky, the colder it gets.
- Clouds are made of **condensed** water vapor.
- Rain is a kind of precipitation.

Ask Questions

- Does ice make water vapor change?
- How does precipitation fall from clouds?

19

Gather Your Supplies!

- Adult help
- A pot of water
- A stove
- Oven mitts
- A bowl with handles
- Ice
- A foil pie tin
- Pencil or pen
- Paper

Make a Prediction

Here are two examples:

- Ice makes water vapor cool and condense.
- Ice does not change water vapor.

Time to Experiment!

1. Fill the bowl with ice.
2. Have an adult do steps 3 to 6. Watch and take notes.
3. Set the pan of water on the stove.
4. Bring the water to a boil.

5. Hold the pie tin high over the boiling water.
6. Hold the bowl of ice over the pie tin.
7. Watch the bottom of the bowl of ice. What falls into the pie tin? Write down what happens.

Review the Results

What did you see? Water appeared on the sides of the bowl with ice. The water drops fell from the bowl into the pie tin.

What Is Your Conclusion?

The small drops of water condensed on the sides of the bowl. The steam was like the water vapor in the air. The bowl of ice was like cool air in the sky. It cooled the steam. The water drops cooled. They condensed into drops on the bowl. In the sky, water vapor condenses into clouds. The drops fell into the pie tin, like precipitation. This is how rain falls to the ground.

Snowflakes form as **crystals** from water vapor in very cold air. Hail is a chunk of ice formed in layers.

CHAPTER SIX

See the Water Cycle

The water cycle goes on and on. It never ends. How does it move in a cycle? Try this to see.

Research the Facts

Here are a few. What other facts do you know?

- You find water in three forms: solid (ice), liquid (water), and gas (water vapor).
- The three main steps of the water cycle are evaporation, condensation, and precipitation.

23

Have you seen condensation on a window?

Ask Questions

- What happens when water is heated by sunlight?
- What happens when water vapor cannot escape into the air?

Make a Prediction

Here are two examples:

- Water will evaporate into the air through the bag.
- Water vapor will be trapped by the bag and become liquid again.

Gather Your Supplies!

- Small paper cup
- Large zippered plastic bag
- Heavy duty tape
- Water
- Pencil or pen
- Paper

Time to Experiment!

1. Fill the cup halfway with water.
2. Put the cup of water into the plastic bag. The cup should be sitting at the bottom of the bag.
3. Close the bag. Let it hold some air.
4. Carefully lift the bag. Do not spill the water.

5. Tape the plastic bag to a window that gets lots of sun.

6. Check the bag every two hours until you go to sleep. Record what you see.

7. Check the bag in the morning. Record the results.

Review the Results

Look over what you wrote. You saw water collect on the bag. The cup is not as full as it was at first. Some of the water dripped down the sides of the bag.

What Is Your Conclusion?

The sun evaporated the water. The water moved into the bag as water vapor. Then it collected onto the bag's sides. This was condensation. Cool air traps water vapor in the sky. In the bag, the closed top trapped the water vapor. It could not rise into the air, so it condensed. When the water drops grew heavy, they fell down the sides of the bag. That was like precipitation. The three steps of the water cycle happened in the bag.

The sun makes water evaporate.

Way to go! You are a scientist now. What fun water cycle facts did you learn? You found out that water moves from the ground to the clouds as water vapor. You saw that water condenses in clouds and falls as precipitation. You can learn even more about the water cycle. Study it. Experiment with it. Then share what you learn about the water cycle.

Glossary

conclusion (kuhn-KLOO-shuhn): A conclusion is what you learn from doing an experiment. His conclusion is that cold temperatures make water vapor condense.

condensation (kon-den-SAY-shuhn): Condensation is water vapor that has been cooled into a liquid. Condensation is seen in the sky as clouds.

condensed (kuhn-DENSSD): When a gas has condensed, it turns into a liquid, usually as a result of cooling. Water condensed on the outside of the glass.

crystals (KRISS-tuhlz): Crystals are a body with many flat surfaces that form when a liquid becomes a solid. Snowflakes are crystals of ice.

evaporates (i-VAP-uh-rates): When a liquid evaporates, it moves into the air as a gas. Water evaporates when it is heated.

experiment (ek-SPER-uh-ment): An experiment is a test or way to study something to learn facts. An experiment can show how the water cycle works.

groundwater (GROUND-waw-tur): Groundwater is water that is in the earth. Some groundwater comes from rain.

precipitation (pri-sip-i-TAY-shun): Precipitation is water that falls from the sky as rain, snow, sleet, or hail. Precipitation falls from the clouds.

prediction (pri-DIKT-shun): A prediction is what you think will happen in the future. His prediction is that water vapor will condense on the glass.

water vapor (WAW-tur VAY-pur): Water vapor is water in the air that cannot be seen. Water vapor condenses into clouds.

Books

Lyon, George Ella, and Katherine Tillotson. *All the Water in the World.* New York: Atheneum Books for Young Readers, 2011.

Peterson, Christine. *A Project Guide to Earth's Waters.* Hockessin, DE: Mitchell Lane Publishers, 2010.

Strauss, Rochelle. *One Well: The Story of Water on Earth.* Toronto: Kids Can Press, 2007.

Index

Web Sites

Visit our Web site for links about water cycle experiments:
childsworld.com/links

Note to Parents, Teachers, and Librarians: We routinely verify our Web links to make sure they are safe and active sites. So encourage your readers to check them out!

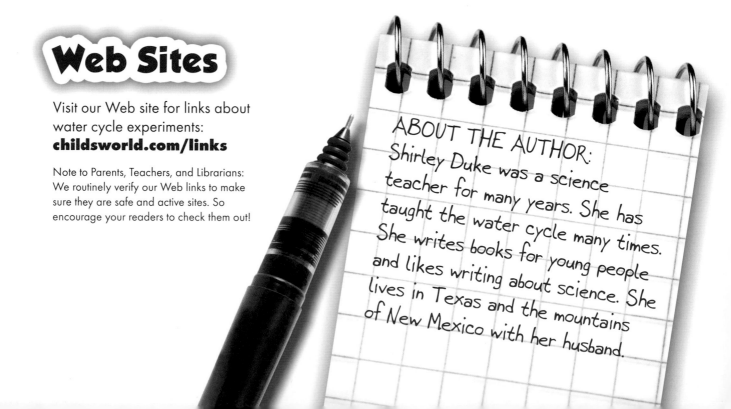

ABOUT THE AUTHOR:
Shirley Duke was a science teacher for many years. She has taught the water cycle many times. She writes books for young people and likes writing about science. She lives in Texas and the mountains of New Mexico with her husband.